# THE GOLDEN TALE

A Goldentail Adventure Story Book

By Dana Marie Hoffmann

Illustrated by Erin O'Leary Brown

The Hoffmann Partnership
Bloomingdale, IL 60108

THE HOFFMANN PARTNERSHIP T.H.P. THE HOFFMANN PARTNERSHIP

# THE GOLDEN TALE

A Goldentail Adventure Story Book

## Author: Dana Marie Hoffmann
## Illustrator: Erin O'Leary Brown

Library of Congress Control Number: 2004092288

ISBN: 0-9753106-0-7   First Edition

Printed in the United States of America

Publisher
The Hoffmann Partnership
Bloomingdale, IL 60108

www.WriteHappy.com

Best Wishes!
Dana '06

On a warm spring day a very special fish was born.
Her long tail shimmered like gold in the early
morning sun. Her parents named her Goldentail.

Goldentail was a happy fish.
She greeted others with a smile and kind words.

When Goldentail started school she knew almost everyone in her class.

Goldentail enjoyed going to school. She learned to count and write the letters of the alphabet.

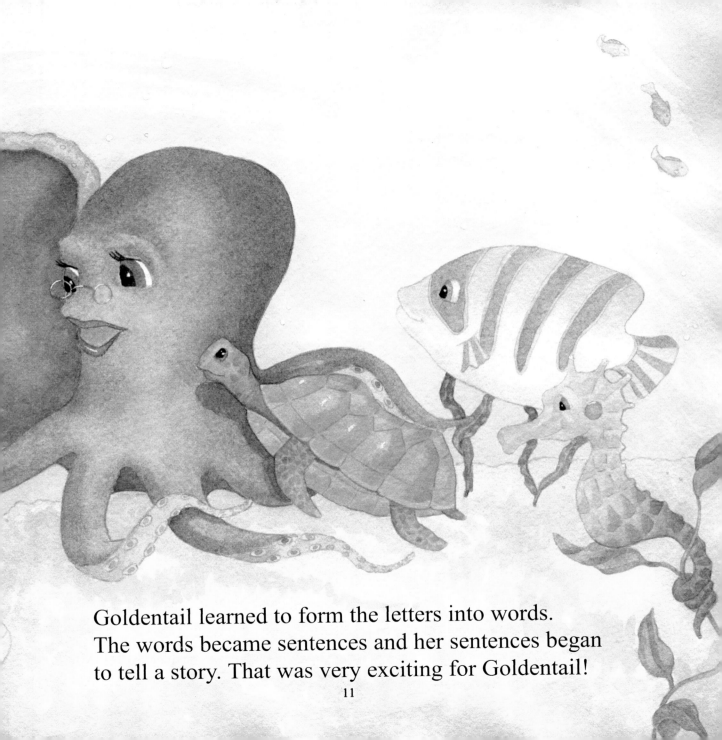

Goldentail learned to form the letters into words.
The words became sentences and her sentences began
to tell a story. That was very exciting for Goldentail!

11

Then Goldentail started her very own
journal so she would remember each day.

She had many grand days, many good days,
some okay days and just a few not-so-okay days.

Goldentail liked to write in her journal every day. Sometimes she wrote pages and pages, sometimes a few sentences and one time she wrote just a word.

One morning while Goldentail, her mother and
two brothers were swimming to school, a large
gray shark suddenly appeared from the dark water.

Startled, the fish fled in separate directions.

Goldentail swam as fast as she could from the shark.

Along the shoreline she saw a tree had fallen in the water. The tree had many tangled branches and Goldentail quickly swam into a small opening among them.

Safely hidden from the shark, she glanced at her tail. It was almost gone!

Exhausted, Goldentail curled up
within the branches and fell asleep.

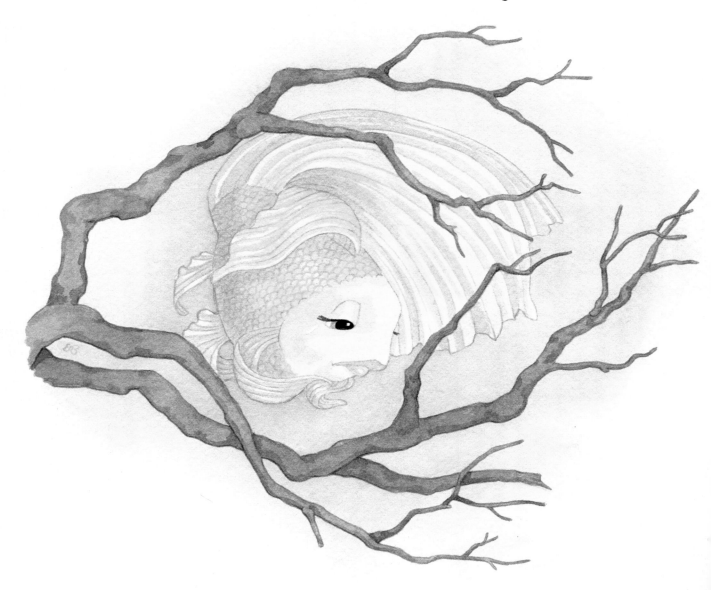

It wasn't long before her dad found her.
She showed him her tail and he
thought everything would be okay.
Together they swam home.

But Goldentail was not okay. She was very
unhappy. The other fish had not asked about
her tail and her terrifying escape from the shark.

They did not seem to notice.

They did not seem to care.

Goldentail was sad. She thought leaving home and going far away would be best.

Not knowing where to go, she swam to the waters' edge to be alone.

"OUCH!" said Goldentail.
The water swirled where she bumped
her head, and a loud, stern voice asked,

"ARE YOU TRYING TO PUSH ME
                    OFF MY LILY PAD?"

Goldentail was scared. She had never seen such a creature; it was green, slimy and covered with spots.

This odd-looking being demanded an explanation. She had disturbed his peaceful rest and he wanted to know the reason.

29

Goldentail sadly told him her story, and that she had planned to leave her home.

She thought no one cared about her and her small tail.

"Nonsense!" bellowed the creature. He then informed her that he didn't even have a tail and was as happy as any frog that just caught a fly for snacking.

# S M A C K!
And that is what he did!
Then the frog laughed.

Goldentail laughed along with her newly found friend with no tail. She thought if he could be happy with no tail then she would be happy with herself too, after all, she could not...

*That was it!*
*That was the one word Goldentail*
*wrote in her journal that day...* change.

Goldentail could not change what the shark
had done to her long beautiful tail, but she could
change the way she would feel about herself.

With that thought in her mind and the change in her heart,
she waved good-bye to the frog and swam home.

Goldentail had changed. Once again she
greeted others with a smile and kind words...

39

...and today Goldentail is a happy fish with many happy memories and stories written in her journal.

The End

# TODAY IS A GREAT DAY TO START YOUR JOURNAL!

Write Happy & Share the Fun!™ is the special way you write your words to create a happy story.

Smile when you write in your journal and your words will tell a HAPPY STORY.

# WRITE HAPPY

## &

## SHARE

## THE FUN!™